TV TREVOR
by TONY GARTH

Trevor spent every spare moment watching television. If he saw a show that he particularly liked he would dress up and pretend to be the main character.

At the moment, Trevor was pretending to be 'Rex the Wonder Dog', and insisting on sleeping in an old basket on his bedroom floor.

Trevor's Mum never knew who he was going to be next.

"Breakfast is ready Trevor," she shouted, the next morning, "served in a dog bowl on the floor, as requested."

Suddenly, a caped super-hero ran into the kitchen. "Good morning Mum," said Trevor, "I'm 'Galactic Kid' and I only eat high energy, galactic neutron bars for breakfast."

Trevor's Mum sighed, "I'll try and buy some today," she said.

Trevor was 'Galactic Kid' all day at school. He saved his friends from imaginary space aliens and flew about at the speed of light.

In the maths lesson he was made to stand in the corner. "It's very strange that someone with a brain more powerful than the largest computer in the galaxy could get such low marks in a maths test," said Mr. Franks. "Why can't you just be yourself?"

Next day, at breakfast, Trevor's Mum was unwrapping galactic neutron bars. "He won't eat those," said Trevor's Dad.

"But these are 'Galactic Kid's' favourite food," she said.

"That may be true," said Dad, "but werewolves only eat meat."

"Werewolves? Oh no!" said Mum, as she remembered that 'Night of the Howlers' had been on TV last night.

They both turned as they heard a howl at the kitchen door. Trevor was standing there. He was wearing plastic teeth and Mum's fur hat and gloves. "Owwwwooooooo..." he said.

Trevor was a werewolf all day at school. He frightened some of the younger children and threatened to eat the school rabbit.

That night he annoyed his parents by standing in the back garden, howling at the moon. "Why can't he just be himself?" they said to each other.

The following morning, Trevor's Mum was ready for him. She had looked through the television magazine and made a choice of breakfasts. There was a programme about chimpanzees so she had bananas. There was a cowboy show so she made beans. You name it, she had it.

"Good morning Mum," said a small robot, as it walked, stiffly, into the room. "No breakfast for me thanks, just a squirt of oil on my knee joints please."

"I give up," said Mum. "He must have watched his 'Robo-Ranger' video.'

Trevor clanked about as a robot all day. He couldn't sit down and he couldn't play football. The teachers were not amused.

That afternoon it began to rain. "I hope I don't rust," thought Trevor.

The weather got much worse and, that evening, there was a huge thunder storm. Trevor had just settled down in front of the TV when, suddenly, everything went off! The lights, the electric clock and, worst of all, the TV!

"Don't worry," said his Dad, as he appeared, holding a torch. "It's only a power cut. The storm must have brought the lines down."

Trevor didn't know what to do with himself. "Who am I going to be tomorrow?" he said.

"You'll just have to be yourself," smiled his Dad.

"This is very nice," said Trevor's Mum, in the morning. "I can't remember the last time you had breakfast as yourself."

Trevor's Dad almost didn't recognise him in his normal clothes.

On the school bus his friends couldn't believe their eyes. "It's Trevor, just being himself!" they laughed.

Suddenly, the bus driver had to swerve around a big branch, blown down by the storm. The bus ended up stuck in a muddy ditch.

Nobody knew what to do - apart from Trevor He ran about gathering twigs, which he put under the wheels. "Try it now," he shouted. The driver started the bus and, in a moment, they were free and back on the road.

The children cheered. "Well done Trevor," said the bus driver, "you saved us, and, for once, you did it as yourself."

"Little do they know," thought Trevor, to himself, "that beneath this disguise as a mild mannered schoolboy, I am in fact 'Cosmic Kid'!"

Collect all 30 titles in the Little Monsters series